Dear Santa
Please, don't come this year

Illustrated by Patricia D. Ludlow

Child's Play (International) Ltd

Swindon   Bologna   New York
© M. Twinn 1993   ISBN 0-85953-778-1   Printed in Singapore

Santa's castle has stood for nearly two thousand years!

Santa's helpers were returning after their well-earned rest.

They gathered in little groups,
their voices tinkling like sleigh bells in the frosty air.
They had so much to tell each other.

"Look!   Here comes Santa!"

"Another
Christmas!"

"It's good to be back!"

"Where did you go?"

"What did you do?"

The dungeons were filled with the gifts
that Chief Helper had ordered from the toymakers...

All the usual games, books, paint sets,
recorders, trains and bikes...

Everything any child could ever want.
Maybe, something for you?

Chief Helper read the list to Santa.

"And, let me see..." said Chief Helper.
"This year, we have five million video games
and ten million computers..."

Santa shook his head.

"I'm too old for computers!
I can't understand them!
And they are so expensive!
You know, Chief, something is missing . . .
I just don't quite know what it is."

Then Santa beamed.
"Ahh! Here come my old friends,
the Teddy bears.
It really is Christmas, after all!"

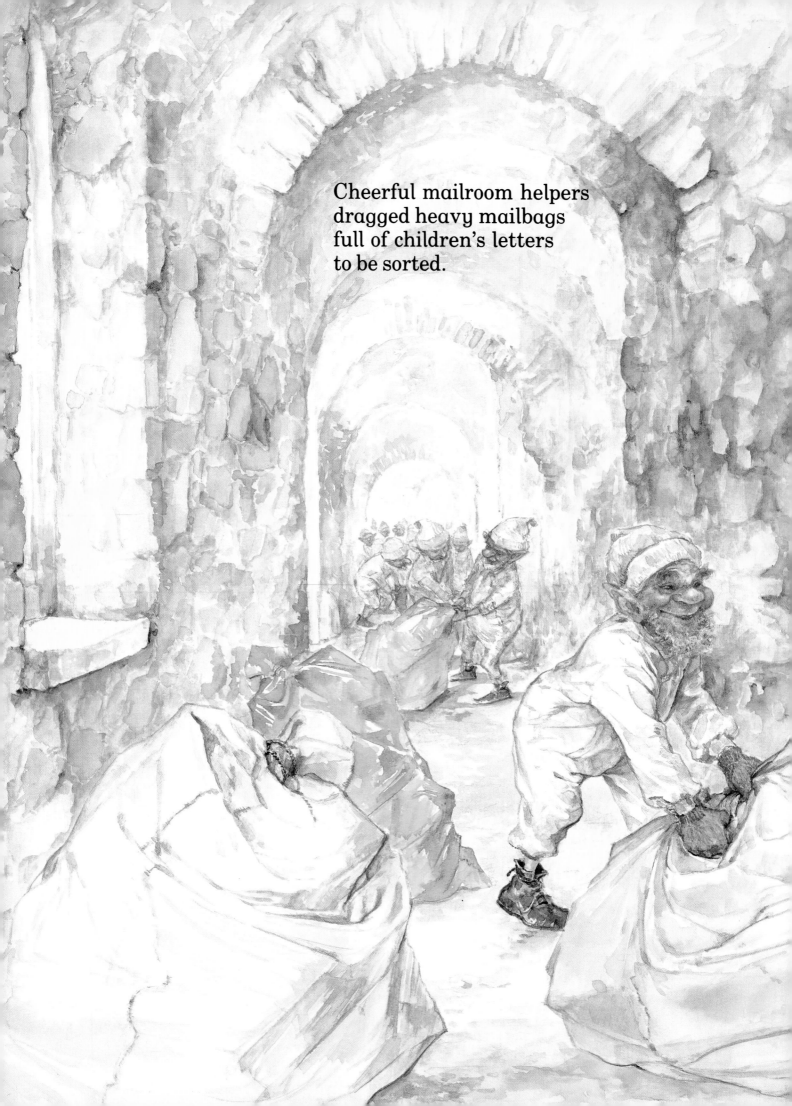

Cheerful mailroom helpers
dragged heavy mailbags
full of children's letters
to be sorted.

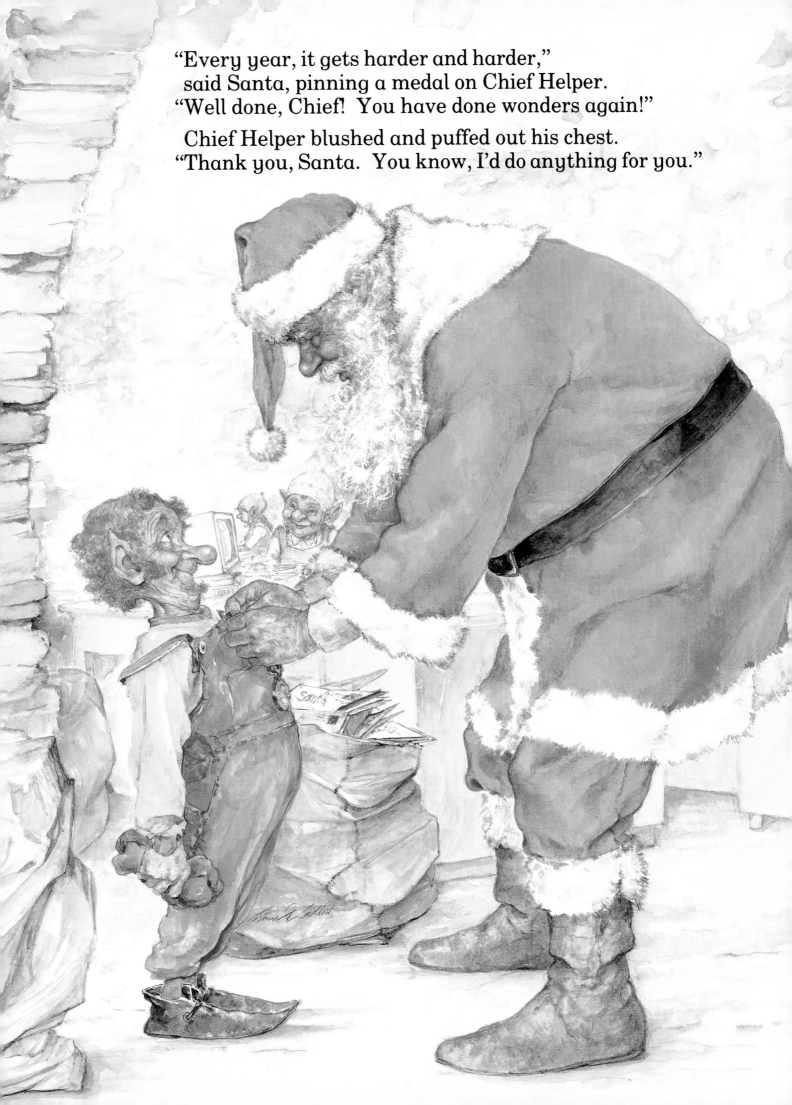

"Every year, it gets harder and harder,"
said Santa, pinning a medal on Chief Helper.
"Well done, Chief! You have done wonders again!"

Chief Helper blushed and puffed out his chest.
"Thank you, Santa. You know, I'd do anything for you."

In the office, Santa's secretaries sorted the requests.
Santa always knows what each child deserves.

It is very hard on his memory these days,
so the new video screens on the walls help a lot.

On one you can see the children and on others
the presents they have asked for.

"...orry, Santa,"
...id Chief Helper.
...ll the children are
...sking for the ugly
...hree-headed dinosaurs
...ey have seen on T.V.
...e are sure to
...un out . . ."

"They'll be just as happy
with Teddy bears,"
said Santa.

But he wasn't sure.
His wrinkled brow
crumpled into a frown.

"I know what I'm getting.
My Dad told m
I don't believ
in Santa Clau

Give me a t
headed dinosa
Give me some
video games.
Give me

Santa looked at the screen and heaved a sigh.

"Listen to this letter, Chief.
No 'Dear Santa', no 'Please'.
Just, 'Give me, give me, give me.'
But the more they get, the less they believe.
Poor kids. It's not their fault. Sometimes, I blame myself."

"I think this will be my last year. I'm getting too old.
Kids have so much now. Christmas isn't what it was.

"I remember my first: one innocent baby born in a stable.
Presents from poor shepherds and three wise men . . .

"Zzzzzzzzz."

Poor Santa!
But just as he was nodding off,
Chief Helper rushed in,
grinning from ear to ear.

"One letter to go, Santa.
The very last one for this year!
It must have taken someone
a long time to write!"

As he read the first line, Santa's face fell.
Then, as he read on, he smiled a smile that lit up
the whole room.

'Dear Santa,
Please, don't come this year.

You always bring us fine presents. Thank you.
But, Santa, we have almost everything we want.

Lots of children don't get presents.
Some don't have enough to eat or anywhere to live.
Some don't have anyone to look after them,
even when they are sick . . .

So, we don't want presents for ourselves this year.
At least, nothing much.
We want to help other children, instead.
And old people and animals in need.

We love you, Santa.

George and the Gang'

"I've been waiting to hear from them," said Santa.
"They always cheer me up. I was worried.
Let's see them on the screen."

e enough
where to live.
ave anyone
them.
t want presents
s this year.
nothing much.
to help other
, instead,
ld people and
als in need.

As they watched the screen,
Santa and Chief Helper
grew more and more excited.

"They mean every word!
They really do!
Those kids are wonderful!
Their parents, too!

"That's it! They're right!
It's been my fault all along.
I've been too soft.
Now I know what I have to do!"

"Why doesn't Santa
visit the children
who don't write to him?
Some are too ill
or too hungry."

"Some are so poor,
they can't afford
a pen."

"Yes, and some don't know how to write.
They don't have a school to go to."

"Santa's kind.
He does whatever children ask.
But he can't do everything by himself.
We have to help, too!"

"Mum, what about animals?
They can't write to Santa."

"... Chief, there is no time to lose.
We must send a message at once."

When the gentle reindeer knew what Santa planned,
they couldn't wait to begin their magic journey.
Even though they knew it might be the last one
they would ever make.

"Parents and grandparents,
aunts and uncles:
I want you to deliver the presents.
Wear my uniform, if you like.

"I am leaving
on a special mission.
Kids today are great.
Especially yours.

"Now, fly reindeer. Fly!"

"Have a good trip, Santa!
We got your message."

The gift of food
The gift of health

Why should babies die?
Why should mothers weep?
Why should some have plenty
and others not enough to eat?

It didn't take the reindeer long to find people
who were sick and hungry. Santa and his helpers
brought them food and medicine.

But he needed much more.

The gift of sight
Eyes are for seeing not for sorrowing.

"These tablets will protect your eyes and your precious gift of sight. Trust me."

The gift of water

There won't be a harvest,
if we don't have water.

Gifts of food are always welcome.
But what about next year?

Santa brought seed to plant.
But he needed more.

"Ohh! My poor old back.
Whatever happened to magic?
This earth is as hard as rock!"

The gift of technology
The gift of hard work

Santa and his helpers searched
for water and dug wells.

But they needed more.

The gift of peace

*We won't grow enough food
or dig enough wells,
if we don't have peace.*

"Peace on Earth!
That's my message every Christmas.
If only we can make it come true!
Why do people fight?"

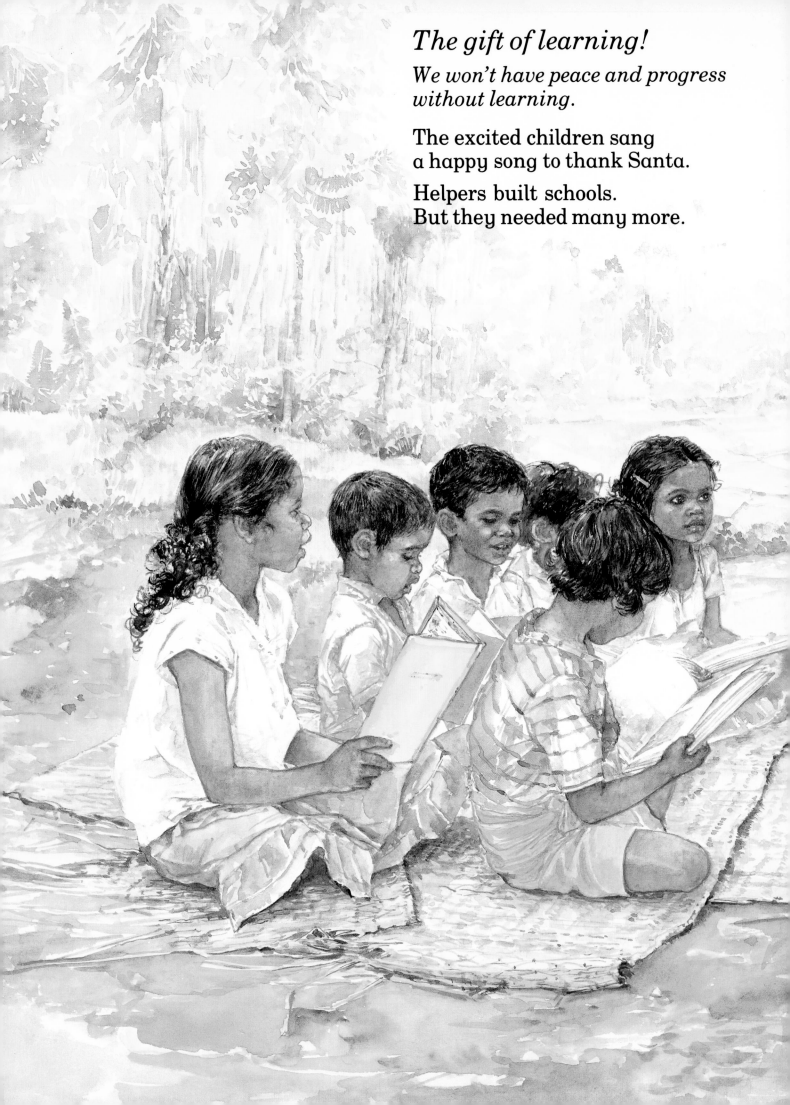

The gift of learning!
We won't have peace and progress
without learning.

The excited children sang
a happy song to thank Santa.

Helpers built schools.
But they needed many more.

"All these years I never realized
what a difference books make.
If only I had brought more."

The gift of survival

We won't enjoy our planet,
if we don't share it with the animals.

"The children want animals to be protected.
Imagine a world without elephants!

"Our wardens will keep ivory poachers at bay
until we find them better work to do.

"Now let's go and take care of the hippos
and rhinos and zebra and all others . . ."

When Santa returned to his castle, he was not alone.

"Welcome, new helpers!
Two of my old friends can retire now!

"There must be many children like you,
who would like to help.
We need more. We need everyone.

"Do you know SOMEONE?"

"A sackful
of thank you letters
for a change!
Will you help me read them?"

"Then you can go
and test all the new toys."

"Do you know, Santa, it used to take you only a day
to visit millions of homes. I had almost a year to get you ready!
Yet, I haven't been looking forward to it at all, recently."

"This trip took nearly a whole year,
but I can't wait to start again!

"Helping others is fun!
Why didn't I see that sooner?
The greatest gift is yourself.

"Now I have an important letter to write."

"Look, gang! A message from Santa! He says:

'Dear Kids,

I never knew how hard it is to write a thank you letter.
This is the first one I've ever had to write!

Thank you for your money and gifts, your time and your love.

You and your families have made so many people happy.

You've brought magic back to Christmas.

I believe in kids, again.
And grown-ups, too.

Love,
Santa.'"